The Otter, the Spotted Frog & the Great Flood: A Creek Indian Story
© 2013 Text Gerald Hausman and Illustrations Ramon Shiloh

The illustrations are rendered in color pencil and ink.

Wisdom Tales is an imprint of World Wisdom, Inc.

Library of Congress Cataloging-in-Publication Data

Hausman, Gerald.
  The otter, the spotted frog & the Great Flood : a Creek Indian story / by Gerald Hausman ; illustrated by Ramon Shiloh.
      pages cm
  ISBN 978-1-937786-12-0 (hardcover : alk. paper) 1. Creek mythology. 2. Creek Indians--Folklore. 3. Legends--Southern
States. I. Shiloh, Ramon, illustrator. II. Title. III. Title: Otter, the spotted frog and the Great Flood.
  E99.C9.H29 2013
  398.208'97385075--dc23

                    2013021089

Printed in China on acid-free paper
Production Date: June, 2013, Plant & Location: Printed by Everbest Printing (Guangzhou, China), Co. Ltd, Job / Batch: # 115599

For information address Wisdom Tales,
P.O. Box 2682, Bloomington, Indiana 47402-2682
www.wisdomtalespress.com

❖ Wisdom Tales ❖

THE OTTER, THE SPOTTED FROG & THE GREAT FLOOD

A CREEK INDIAN STORY

by GERALD HAUSMAN
Illustrated by RAMON SHILOH

For Lorry, my Listener. ~ G.H.

For my mother June (Sukuybtet),
who always wanted a book published.
We did it. Rest in Peace. ~ R.S.

DAY ONE

There were two animal people who lived in the long ago.

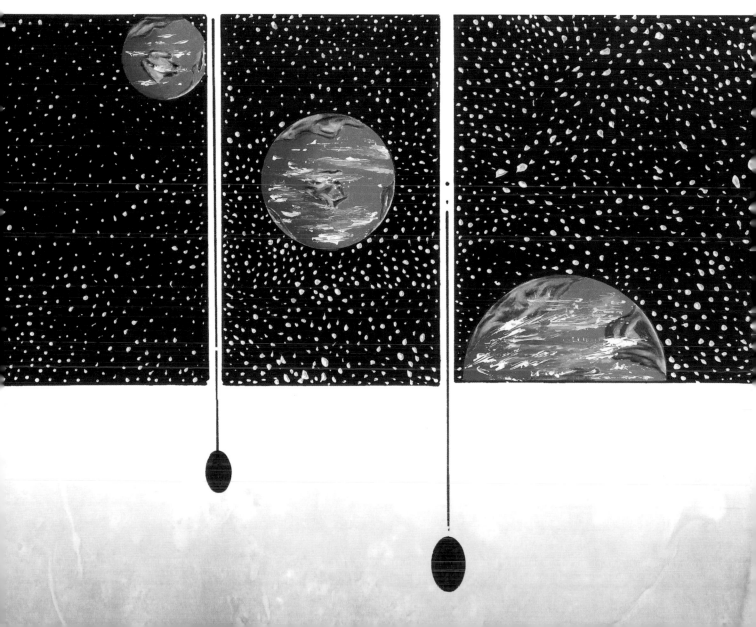

One was Listener, a river otter.

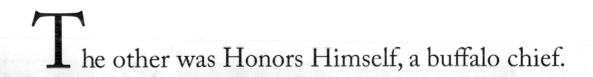

The other was Honors Himself, a buffalo chief.

They lived in a village by a great swamp.
At night the frogs sang in many voices, but only one of the animal people listened to them, and that was Listener, the Otter.

"I hear many frogs," he said one night as he sat by his fire.

Honors Himself, who was there too, said, "I do not like frogs."

Listener left his warm place by the fire and he went into the wet woods. There he found Spotted Frog and brought him back to the fire.

"This is the one who sings above the others," Listener said.

"Why do you do that?" Honors Himself asked the little frog.

"I sing the prophecy," said Spotted Frog.

Honors Himself took Spotted Frog by the neck, and tossed him into the fire.

"That was a bad thing to do," Listener said. And he fetched the frog out of the flames.

Spotted Frog sat on Listener's knee, and it was as if the flames had not touched him.

Honors Himself pushed Spotted Frog back into the flames. This happened four times.

And each time Listener got Spotted Frog out of the fire.

But after the fourth time, the frog sang out: "A Great Flood is coming. Soon it will cover the land. I sing so you can save yourselves."

Honors Himself snorted. Returning to the meadow where he and his people lived, he thought no more of frogs, floods, or fools.

Listener, however, kept listening.

He asked Spotted Frog: "Tell me again about the Great Flood."

"In the time to come," said Spotted Frog, "the water will cover the land. Even a strong swimmer like yourself will grow weary of swimming and eventually you will drown with the others. So you must build a raft. Tie it together with hickory rope. Then tether it to the tallest water oak tree in the woods. When the flood comes, you will float up into the sky. The rope will keep you from floating away into the Forever."

Day 2

L istener made the raft and braided the rope, and while he worked Otter Woman came to see him. She had heard of the Great Flood.

O tter Woman asked Listener, "What are you doing?"

"I am doing what Spotted Frog told me to do. I am preparing for the Great Flood."

"I see no flood," she said.

"The Great Flood will come. That is what Spotted Frog said."

"There is not a cloud in the sky," Otter Woman said.

"Don't you believe me?" he asked.

"I want to believe you," she said. "But Honors Himself, the buffalo chief, says that nothing will happen. He says not to listen to you." After a time, she went away.

Then Honors Himself came by. "I see no flood," he said.

"What do you see?" Listener asked.

"I see a fool who listens to a frog."

Listener did not say anything.

After a while, Honors Himself went away, laughing to himself.

But soon all the animal people told funny stories about the Great Flood. They laughed at Listener and Spotted Frog.

Listener paid no attention to them.

"I have done what you told me to do," Listener said to Spotted Frog. "What shall I do now?"

Spotted Frog told Listener, "You must press bitter grass and moss into the cracks of the raft. Then the beaver people won't chew on the rope and gnaw on the logs."

Listener listened. He got some grass and moss and pressed them neatly into the chinks of the logs.

Then Spotted Frog told him, "Tie the hickory rope around the tallest water oak in the woods. The Great Flood will come soon and the water will be deep and strong."

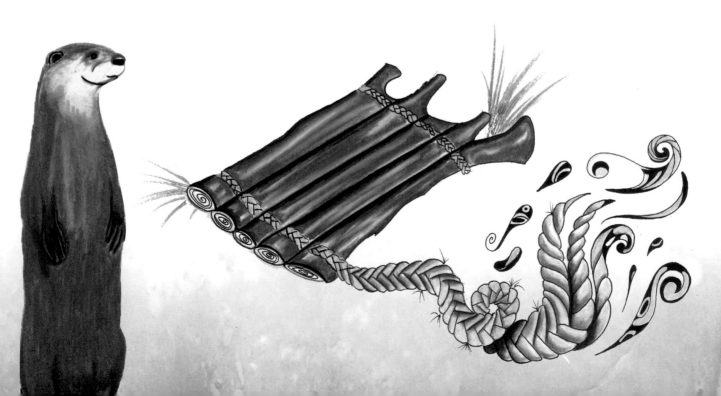

By day's end, the rain came. The swamp swelled and the rivers filled and the waters rose on the banks. In the night the rain was harder and the land ran with many rivers that formed a great lake.

On the high ground meadow, Honors Himself gathered the animal people and said, "This will soon pass. You will see."

But the water kept rising and the great lake grew larger.

Listener could do nothing for the animal people who had done nothing for themselves.

He was riding out the floodwaters on his raft and they, the animal people who would not listen to Spotted Frog, were paddling in the muddy waters.

Now the waters ran higher and higher and after a time
they covered even the tallest water oak in the land.
The animal people were soon swept away in the Great
Flood and still the floodwaters rose.

Listener wondered about Otter Woman, and he looked for her, but he did not see her. He stayed on his raft, and the rain came down and the waters went up and Listener floated to the dome of the sky.

There his raft stopped. The hickory rope, longer than any in the world, stayed rooted to the oak.

Far below in the gloom, fish flew like silent birds through the sunken trees. Alligators and manatees swam through the silence of the deepening flood.

The bird people, who had nothing left to hang on to, hooked their claws into the bright dome of the sky. Holding on, upside down, the waters soaked the birds' tails. The colors ran together so that Hawk's brown tail turned red and Turkey's dark tail tip turned foam-white. And these are the colors that they have today.

DAY THREE

On the third day, the waters began to go down.

Spotted Frog came by, and hopped on Listener's raft.

"Listener, my friend," he said, "you will soon be alone in the mud of the new world."

"Am I the only otter person left?"

"That is so."

"What should I do now?" Listener asked.

"Remember your name."

And Spotted Frog jumped off and swam away.

When the waters went away, Listener sat on his raft and looked upon the land.

The sky was gray and the earth was brown.

Listener listened.

"What is that whining noise I hear?"

Listener listened some more.

The whining noise seemed to come from all six directions.

"It comes from everywhere . . . and nowhere," Listener said to himself.

The whining noise did not stop.

But after a while Listener stopped listening.

"Maybe it is the noise of the new world," he said.

That night Spotted Frog came to the raft.

Listener had not moved.

"How are you, my friend?"

"The world is not the same," Listener said.

"You will not be alone much longer."

Listener wondered about this.

When he looked around, Spotted Frog was gone.

"Wait, I want to ask you something."

The whining noise grew louder.

L istener shook his head.

Now the noise seemed to come from within his ear. "Who's there?"

A thin, little voice cried, "Oh, my husband."

"Where are you?" asked Listener. "Who are you?"

"Here," the voice whined. "I am yours."

Listener felt something on his arm. It was a person with a long nose, bowlegs, and clear wings.

"Why do you say, 'Oh, my husband'?" Listener asked.

The long-nosed person said, "Before the Great Flood, I was Otter Woman and I had a dream in which, one day, I would marry someone handsome whose name was Listener."

"That is my name."

"Then it was you that I dreamed about. But now, as you see, I am Mosquito Woman."

"How do you live?"
"I drink blood," she answered.

Listener thought about it.

Then he asked her, "What happened to all the animal people?"

"They turned into starving mosquitoes like me," she said.

Listener said, "I don't really want a mosquito wife. But I am lonely, so perhaps a mosquito wife is better than no wife at all."

DAY FOUR

"You may stay with me if you wish," Listener said. This made Mosquito Woman dance about in the air.

L istener tried to sleep but he could not do so with the noise of her voice. In the morning he bathed in the lake and he was surprised by his reflection. All over his body there were red bites.

"Wife, can this really be me?" he cried.

"It is you, husband," Mosquito Woman said.

The next morning, when he saw his face in the lake, he didn't know himself. "I look thin and pale, like all the blood has run out of me. Wife, there's something wrong with me."

"Are you sick, husband?"

"I feel weak," Listener said.

"Husband, I know what is wrong. When I crawl into your ear to sleep, I drink some of your blood. I am always well fed, but you, poor husband, you get nothing to eat."

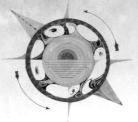

"I'm very hungry," Listener said, "but I'm not strong enough to find food."

"I will get something for you, husband," Mosquito Woman said. She dipped her long nose into the lake. In no time, a fish took hold of it. She danced upwards, whirring her wings. Then she pulled the fish onto the earth.

"Here, husband," she said. "Now you shall eat."

Listener felt better after eating the fish. But soon, he was weak again. "Wife," he said, "you must have drunk too much of my blood—I feel sick."

"I will catch another fish," she said, and once again Mosquito Woman dipped her long nose into the lake, but this time a great fish leaped into the air, and swallowed her whole.

Dragging himself to the water's edge, Listener saw the fish that had just eaten his wife. Angry, he grabbed the fish by the tail and pulled it on to dry land. "Fish," he said, "you've killed my wife, and now I am going to eat you."

"No," said a voice. It was Spotted Frog.

"Do not kill a pretty woman," he warned.

"What pretty woman?" Listener asked.

The fish, lying on its side, gasped, "Husband, do you not see?"

Listener heard Mosquito Woman's voice speaking from the fish's mouth.

But the fish melted in the sun, and was gone.

"Oh, my precious wife," Listener said. "You're not here with me anymore."

"Husband, do you not like me better now?"

Listener looked up. A lovely two-legged woman stood before him.

"That is Otter Woman who watched you build your raft," Spotted Frog said. "And look at you!"

Listener looked at his feet and saw that he had become a two-legged man.

"Oh, my husband," Listener's wife said. "You are now like me. We are both two-legged. You are handsome . . . and I am—"

"—First Woman, and that is what I shall call you from this day forward," Listener said.

"But I must say, I loved you even when you were Mosquito Woman and you drank my blood."

And that is how First Man and his wife, First Woman, came to be the first two-leggeds born into this world. The earth was good to them, so they say, and they were good to the earth in return. And they always listened to Spotted Frog, who as everyone knows, saved the world by singing.

AUTHOR'S NOTE

The Otter, the Spotted Frog & the Great Flood is an origin tale of the Georgia Creek Indians, ancestors of the Florida Seminole and Miccosukee tribes.

Native versions of a Great Flood story are not unusual and it is also not surprising that the native storyteller may have heard some parts of Genesis and woven a little of this into the tale. The Creeks had trade and other such relations with Scottish settlers; the Indians much admired the Scots' style of dress—kilts, capes, and headdresses—and their oral tradition as well.

The skillful teller of this origin tale may have liked the European moral element in the story, and he may have seen how appropriately it fit with the story he knew and told.

In the end, the tale depends not upon cleverness, but upon our ability to respond to Mother Earth's messages. Artist Ramon Shiloh gives a telling hint of this in the spectral Mound Builders' landscape—they built up, for a reason. Water would come, as it had in the past, as it would in the future.

In the Navajo version of *Otter*, the deity that presides over all water-sources is Water Monster. Coyote steals her babies, which precipitates the Great Flood. It is ended by Coyote's return of the babies.

In the Northwestern Tsimshian story, Little Hawk saves the day with a prayer feather that has four markings: planted on a mountain top, the feather's fourth mark is where the rising water stops.

In the Creek tale, it is Listener, the faithful river otter, who listens to small Spotted Frog, the prophet, and prepares for the worst that is to come. Together the two of them presage the future world of two-leggeds. In all of these stories, the progress is from a lower world to a higher one. In the upper world, there is light, and the possibility for greater and more abundant life.

Interestingly, the message is much the same in all the Great Flood stories I have collected. There is no one way of telling that transcends another and I have heard it said, "There is no competition in tribal storytelling. Just the message and the ways it can be expressed."